To Emma, who made a great little bunny
—L.M.

Library of Congress Cataloging-in-Publication Data
Berlin, Irving, 1888–1989
  Easter parade / by Irving Berlin ; illustrated by Lisa McCue.
     p.   cm.
  Summary: In an illustrated version of the song, a little bunny and her father enjoy
the Easter parade.
  ISBN-10: 0-06-029125-7 (trade bdg.) — ISBN-13: 978-0-06-029125-9 (trade bdg.)
  ISBN-10: 0-06-029126-5 (lib. bdg.) — ISBN-13: 978-0-06-029126-6 (lib. bdg.)
  ISBN-10: 0-06-443720-5 (pbk.) — ISBN-13: 978-0-06-443720-2 (pbk.)
  1. Children's songs—United States—Texts. [1. Songs. 2. Rabbits—Songs and
music. 3. Easter—songs and music.] I. McCue, Lisa, ill.
II. Title.
PZ8.3.B4565 Eas 2003   2001024967
782.42164'0268—dc21
[E]   CIP
                                                                        AC

Typography by Jeanne L. Hogle
❖

Easter Parade

By Irving Berlin ✦ Illustrated by Lisa McCue

HarperCollinsPublishers

Never saw you look
Quite so pretty before;
Never saw you dressed
Quite so lovely, what's more,

I could hardly wait
　To keep our date
　　This lovely Easter morning,
　　　And my heart beat fast
　　　　As I came through the door,
　　　　　For . . .

In your Easter bonnet

With all the frills upon it

You'll be the grandest lady
In the Easter Parade.

I'll be all in clover

And when they look you over

I'll be the proudest fellow

In the Easter Parade.

On the Avenue, Fifth Avenue,

The photographers will snap us,

And you'll find that you're in the rotogravure.

Oh, I could write a sonnet

About your Easter bonnet

And of the girl I'm taking to
The Easter Parade.

Easter Parade

Words and Music by
IRVING BERLIN

Nev-er saw you look   Quite so pret-ty be - fore;_____   Nev-er saw you dressed   Quite so love-ly, what's